Published by Ad Hoc Fiction.
www.AdHocFiction.com

Purchasing Information:
Paperback available from www.AdHocFiction.com
E-book available from all usual outlets.

Printed in the United Kingdom.
First Printing 2021.

ISBN paperback 978-1-912095-24-7
ISBN e-Book 978-1-912095-25-4

The Evolution of Birds

by

Sara Hills

AdHoc Fiction

For Sonora, Kaleia, and Fionniain
For Thomas

Contents

The Evolution of Birds

Hope was the first girl to whittle an arrow and erect a lean-to with foraged brush; the first and only one to get the fire started by means of a cobbled-together bow drill—a strung-up stick whirled fast and hot in the shallow groove of a wooden plate.

But, even though this was Survival Camp, she refused to shoot pigeons.

Ask her to, and she bucked—said she can't. *Won't.*

Hope wiped the charred grease of the fire from her face, her long brown hair hanging limp over her eyes like a defeated warrior, while the camp leader arched his bow and showed the rest of us how to shoot straight. Told us to aim for the breast.

We shot at targets first, red outlines of bird bodies on tacked up paper. Honed our determination and consistency. Learned not to blink.

Then we set loose upon real birds, forgetting to wait until their sleek gray bodies turned toward us. Our aim distracted by the iridescent flash of purple and green on their necks and the far-away sound of their throated coos as they stretched and darted their heads, checking for danger.

"Get inside the bird's head," the leader told us. "Think its thoughts—if it has any. Predict its responses. Detect the slightest effort to flee."

The leader was a real hunter. He slung his kill back to the fire pit where he plucked, gutted and trussed. Showed us how to twist off the wings with a pair of pliers; how to angle the knife blade, slide it up and part the breast. Separate organs from muscle, identify innards and outers. Said only sissies look away.

Depending on the age of the bird, the leader said, it would be skewered, roasted or stewed. We sat around the fire pit while he cooked his kill, steaming the air with the antidote to our hunger. But he didn't share. The leader made us watch while he chewed with his mouth open.

"You want something," he said, "you take it."

We broke into small teams and slithered through the high weeds. We hopped barbed-wire fencing, circled around silver birch and sycamore, and skirted the edge of an abandoned barn.

Wherever we found pigeons, we let loose with a storm of arrows.

Our team bagged three, and between us we feasted like kings, all except Hope.

She said she didn't eat meat because she knew the evolution of birds. "Once upon a time," she told us, "we all crawled out of the sea together. First we were fish, then lizards, then we took to the trees and air."

Hope pointed to the rusted red under our fingernails, the pink flesh on our tin plates, and called it blood lust. She asked what gave us the right.

Survival of the fittest. Isn't that what Darwin always went on about?

The next day we went back out with our bows, learned to be more exacting, pickier, I guess.

"If you want to be sure you've got tender meat," the leader said, "go for the ones with skinny legs."

We all looked at Hope then. I don't know why.

When the leader left our team to it, we forced Hope to take part—goaded her on.

"Do it," we chanted, our breath on her neck.

We didn't give her a choice.

With shaking hands, she held her bow taut and took aim. Her arrow was off by a foot.

When the lucky bird rose up in flight, we weren't far behind.

This is How it Starts

1.

When I open my legs to Lee Jacobs in the cab of his father's pickup, pink sky blooming around the old farm track, I'm not thinking about tomorrow or what my mama would say. Lee whispers, "I love you," against my neck—buttons popping, mouths hot—and I'm not thinking at all.

It's over quickly. Lee's features change from shock to slack. He studies the grooves in the steering wheel cover while I dab at the damp spot between my legs.

"You're back early," Mama says. "Everything all right?"

2.

Everyone's heard about the Plinth girl, how she arrived late to school with a dirt-streaked face and ripped stockings. Said she'd been attacked by three older boys. It was her word against theirs, and when her daddy found out, he beat her.

After the birth, an older couple from Tallahassee tucks the swaddled baby into the back of a station wagon, and the Plinth girl cuts her wrists.

Daddy reads about it in the paper, says to Mama, "She should have kept her legs shut."

3.

Four-year-old Kyra sticks out her tongue, says she doesn't need no babysitter.

Kyra puppets her plastic dolls under the edge of the sofa, while above, Lee traces his fingers under the hem of my skirt.

"Not here," I say.

I haven't told him that I'm twelve days late.

Lee thumbs the elastic edge of my underwear and tells Kyra to go play in her room. "I ain't gotta listen to you," she says. "You're not the boss of me."

She throws her dolls and hits him square in the chest.

He says, "Kids are the worst."

4.

When I tell Aunt Raye, she says this is how it starts. A few hungry kisses too many and good girls turn bad.

She carries my things to her spare room and puts them away. A drawer for me and a drawer for baby. She fluffs the pillows and turns down the blankets. Tells me not to worry. Says time and Jesus will sort things out.

5.

Lee's dead mother drags him to the hospital. The hospital looks like a schoolroom which turns into Aunt Raye's kitchen which turns into a post office. Someone tells me I've got mail.

Mama braids flowers in my hair. I stand on the bed, a white sheet draped around me, and the doctor slips a diamond as big as a cantaloupe on my finger. He tells me I'm beautiful.

The nurse is pregnant. Lee hands her a bouquet of wildflowers, yellow and pink. Aunt Raye tells the nurse, "This is how it starts," and Daddy says she should have kept her legs shut.

The Plinth girl comes to the counter. She pulls plastic dolls from her mouth and asks why we're all here. She asks why nobody believed her. She asks the doctor to sew her wrists. To make her new again.

I dab at the wetness between my legs.

And I hand her the baby.

Pill Babies

My brother Benny dares me to eat my babies. He promises me a dollar for each one. I don't want to eat them, but I say seven dollars would buy me a plastic doll like the other girls have. One that pees and bats her eyes.

I remove the damp log and place the woodlice in my palm. Their bodies roly-poly into little pills.

"Shhh," I say, sounding just like Mama. "No one's gonna hurt you."

I open my mouth and drop one in quick. Real quick for a real baby. It curls up on my tongue and I swear I hear it crying. It pops between my teeth, like wax-covered candy. Only dirt-flavored.

Benny cackles, mouth wide, squealing like a rusty hinge. His molars are dark, packed in chocolate. Chocolate he didn't share with me.

I gag and spit the mangled baby into the dirt.

"Not like this," I say.

We take the babies into the kitchen and heat a slice of butter in a pan. When it's yellowy good and sizzling, I squinch my face and drop one in. It pills when it hits the heat, snaps, then relaxes open. We sauté them, one by one, and spread them on a plate.

"D-d-d-dig in," Benny says. The whatchamacallit on his neck bobs up and down, like he's swallowing for me.

Benny doesn't have seven dollars, and we both know it. The only baby we'll get is the one Mama's cooking in her belly from Mr. Ryarson. The baby that caused Daddy to drink a bottle of whiskey, call Benny the r-word and hold Benny's ear to the stove.

"Are you ready, Benny?" I ask.

His eyes light into a grin and he squeals, clapping joyously, as I take the first bite.

A Piteraq is an Avalanche of Wind

When Bellamy first tastes the power of the wind, she's six. She crouches in the closet, her parents curling around her like a shield. Outside, the wind uproots the copse of silvery-blue pines. It chews the chinquapin oak in half and hurls the green canopy, Bellamy's tire swing and all, through the window and onto the faded blue carpet.

At age eight, the shutters bang like gunshots. Mama says it's only the wind, but the sound penetrates. It enters the house, shouting and cursing up the stairwell. It shakes the hinges on the front door, shaking Mama out with it.

At twelve, Bellamy studies the winds of the world, searching for clues about Mama. Whenever Daddy talks of Mama his tongue flakes with ice, like the Bise, Tramontana, and Mistral—the chill-bringing winds of Europe.

Bellamy sleeps with the window cracked, reciting the names of winds like sheep in the stony silence. She stops at Wreckhouse, wondering if the wind that took Mama had a name like that.

At fourteen, Bellamy finds a hidden polaroid of Mama, mouth loose and bare back arched like a sapling in a fresh gale. In the mirror, Bellamy traces her own contours, mimicking Mama's bend and sway. Bellamy wets her lips and recites the heat-bringing winds like an incantation—Leste, Foehn, Sirocco.

At fifteen, Daddy comes home early and finds Bellamy with a boy between her legs. Daddy's cheeks redden and puff, anger swelling like a piteraq, an avalanche of wind. Bellamy crouches on the floor, curling her hands around herself like a shield.

At sixteen, Bellamy folds gum wrappers into pinwheels and welcomes boys through her open window. Together, they rattle the windowpanes and climax like gunshots.

When Daddy asks, Bellamy tells him it was only the wind. It doesn't feel like lying.

At seventeen, she stands at the mirror and traces her contours, cradling the arc and swell of her changing form. The air stirs inside her, fluttering, soft as a zephyr.

Bellamy packs a bag, and when the wind picks up, she's gone—Mama's polaroid pressed in her back pocket like a destination.

How to Tell a Scary Story

Start with setting

Think about someplace you know. A lonely walk to school, the back alleyways downtown, the dark crevices under the high school bleachers, a house from your childhood. Remember the sodium-yellow haze over the empty parking lot that time in college when a rugby player refused to get out of your car, and decide, instead, to catch the reader off-guard. Think about places that should be more comforting and familiar—a clean ribbon of asphalt under a cloudless sky, the upstairs bathroom at a family Christmas party, a sleepover at your best friend's house, a city bus.

Add in the sounds—the cheering crowd, the seventeenth rendition of Jingle Bells pounded on the piano by your niece, a sharp inhale through a cigarette, a coffined silence, the steady drip from a leaky tap; the smells—pine toilet cleaner, car exhaust, whiskey and vomit, buttered popcorn—know you'll come back to these details later and wonder which ones are worth telling.

Choose a protagonist

Pick someone likable, sympathetic; or not. A small girl whose yellow sundress tickles the tops of her knees, a teenager in torn jeans on her way home late from school. Make her 32, a spinster, a mother. Make her thin as a mint Girl Scout cookie. Make her fat with thighs that rub together under her skirt. Give her glasses or a briefcase, let her clothes inform the time period—a chunky bow in her hair says 1983, a Holly Hobby lunch box says 1979, a flannel shirt and ripped jeans say grunge, 1992. Make her proud or shy, make her a cookie-baking grandmother of four, or a boy with gapped teeth and a hole in his heart. A widower with three children at home. Make them hungry, unsuspecting, naive. Make them a little bit like you. Make them kind to kittens and afraid of breaking the rules. Or not.

Craft a villain

Surprise the reader; make them nonthreatening, approachable. Make them a teacher with a drawer full of snacks, a benevolent uncle, the older brother of your best friend. Remember drunk teenage boys in dark houses, fathers addicted to pills, neighbors with a new game to play. Pluck them out of thin air.

Give them a uniform—a police officer, a postman, a soldier, a doctor, a nurse. Think about the possibility of female villains. Controlling mothers who can reduce a child to the size of a tick with one glance, ready to pop you if they hear one more distasteful word. Angry teachers who make you call them 'Miss' and send you to sit in the hallway for being helpful. Decide it could be any one of them.

Choose a weapon

Start with what you know. Remember your mother's pinched face and her open palm, your brother's fists, your dad's loaded pistol in the bedside table. Remember the boy who chased you home from school with a big stick, how fast you ran. Think legendary weapons—Thor with his mighty hammer, Medusa's eyes, Midas's touch—and wonder about touch as a weapon. Remember all the times your blood felt like it had stopped, clotted to stone, how your legs didn't move—couldn't. Think of celebrities' accusers, think of girls in alleyways behind dumpsters, think of machetes and acid and knife attacks and bombs, and think how easy it would be to go quickly. Think of an unexpected weapon, the thing most villains have in common. Write 'penis.'

Employ rising action. Quicken the pace.

Let your mind rest on the crocheted doll on the back of the toilet, her plastic smile, the exploded lunchbox with the blue thermos rolling into the bushes, the white-and-pink globs of bubble gum pressed under the bleachers, the empty beer cans, chocolate wrappers, the posters of boy bands on the walls. Recall the smells, you always do, the sound of laughter, disparaging remarks. Try not to cry.

The denouement

After, let your protagonist live. Fasten the memory like a tiny shadow tucked inside a heart, a womb, until it gnaws its way out. Let them tell no one what happened, or let them tell everyone. Have them whisper it to their diary, their best friend, their mother. Try to remember how the shards of words can catch in a throat; seeing yourself reflected in your mother's eyes when you told her—how distorted you felt, how dirty, how broken—and make your protagonist look away. Crimson their skin with shame until it feels bruised. Let them pray for help, for forgiveness, for death, for justice that never ever comes.

Let no one believe them.

Let it happen again.

Always Down a Dirt Road, I'm Walking

my two daughters with me. There are trees to the right of us and a field on our left. The field is cropped, oven-crisped at midday. It's hot. Bright.

Then it isn't.

A car whizzes past in a pall of dust, and I pull my youngest daughter out of the road. She's twelve—lanky, absent-minded, unafraid. The other one is quiet, pebble small.

Our dusty sandals slap the loose surface as we continue down the road. Other cars whiz past, but one doesn't. It doesn't.

It rolls to a stop. The window winds down—the sound and intention clear.

"What do we have here?"

In this version, I have daughters. In other versions, sons. In every version, a dirt road, a farm road. There are trees to the right and a field to the left. The trees are straggled juniper. The cropped field, brown and stubble sharp. Further in the distance is our destination—the main road. Blacktop.

The black car window winds down. The dusted door opens to silver-tipped boots, jeans, the smell of sunbaked leather. I pull my daughters close, but they drift apart. Sun flashes on metal. Trees sway. A wax of midday dust settles on my daughters, on me. The grit on my tongue, stubble sharp.

In one version my sons stand tall as trees, juniper jawed, while cars whiz past. My sons spit into the road, chew stalks until they're shorn and soft. In another, my daughters grow straggly and sharp; they remain unafraid. In one version, I cannot hear my heartbeat. In one version, no one is screaming. In one version, we walk through the field. The blacktop before us, trees to our right, and the dark car whizzes past.

It doesn't stop.

Lions in the Amazon

Telling fortunes usually takes fifteen minutes, longer if a ghost turns up, and all night if there's more than one.

Mama reminds me and Charlie to stay in our room, but we already know the drill; if we keep our mouths shut and the door locked, the ghosts won't find us.

I wait for Mama's heel clops to fade down the hallway before I switch on the flashlight. Charlie climbs into my lap, and I take out the worn red atlas, borrowed from the school library. We close our eyes, open the book, and point.

We go to Marrakech and walk the marketplace. Haggle over prices, buy camels and rainbow-colored pots. We go to a fountain in Rome, an empty highway in Mexico, an alleyway in Brazil.

We pretend Mama's laughter is a dance party and the steady squeak through the vent is rats.

Charlie's stomach grumbles, and I rub his belly round and round.

"There will be milk and cereal in the morning," I whisper. "If there are enough ghosts, maybe sugar cereal all week."

We flip the page to a little house in the tundra.

"We could have a goat and milk it every morning," Charlie says.

"The wind is so cold we'd have to wear thick wool hats and at least three sweaters."

"Could Mama tell fortunes there?"

"No," I say. "There wouldn't be any customers for miles. But we'd learn to saw holes in the ice and sing until fish jump out of the water onto our plates."

"What kind of fish?" Charlie asks.

"Silver salmon as big as your leg."

I want to believe in this story. I want to shut out the moans that storm through the vent. The ghosts of men that sometimes take the money in Mama's bedside table and leave bruises across her arms and cheeks.

An angry ghost can keep us out of school all week.

We turn the page and we're in Africa with soldiers carrying guns. They aren't any older than the boys at school. Boys who whisper about saving up for the kind of fortunes Mama tells. Boys who laugh and ask if I read fortunes too.

Charlie traces his finger across the page. "Is there a war?"

"There's always a war somewhere," I say.

He turns to the Amazon and we row along the wide brown river. Pretend the squawking noises are scarlet macaws, that the pounding comes from our own hearts as we race downriver past the hungry cayman, pull at the oars, passing vampire fish and piranha, pull past eel and anaconda, pull and race and pound.

"We're not scared," I tell Charlie. "Not of the water snakes or biting fish."

"Or the lions," Charlie says.

There are no lions in the Amazon, but I know what he means as the sound slows through the vent, how it always feels as if there's something lurking in the shadows. Something wild and dangerous.

The vent goes quiet, and Charlie whispers, "Do you think there are cannibals?"

"Where'd you hear that word?"

Charlie shrugs, so I turn to the pages with islands—faraway places with names like Polynesia and Madagascar. He searches for evidence, but I don't need a picture to imagine it.

I see humans eating humans. Licking the remains off a femur and drinking water from a foam white skull.

Safety in Numbers

"Not one lick of buttercream," Mama warns. "The cake is for the party."

Simi bites her tongue before it talks back.

Turning four means helping scrub her brother's stiff grey socks. Four for starting school. Four, the number of probing fingers on Uncle Pachy's right hand.

Simi glares at the cake until her eyes water. She pokes it. Buttercream gives way, knuckle-deep, and Simi bores four even holes.

She pictures herself in the schoolyard, morning light sunbursting on the windowpanes, disappearing in a clatter of uniformed children. The safety in numbers.

Simi scoops up buttercream and takes a bite.

Nothing by Halves

That's what Ms. Watson said that first week of school when you kept skinning your knees playing hopscotch; when you clambered fast up the only tree in the playground and claimed it as your own. You converted your tree 'house' into a castle; classmates into commoners; commoners into friends. You fought to keep the boys out of our base, fought to keep us girls locked in—safe—and before the bell rang, you wrote your name in large spiky letters, formed from dried ocotillo branches, laid out on the hard-packed earth.

In summer you became the barefoot girl, wading into deep puddles after monsoons swept the desert with rain. You caught tadpoles in a red plastic cup and filled the sun tea jar I collected from my mother's kitchen. You weren't worried what was under that murky water. You weren't even afraid of getting hit in tetherball or going against boys in a dirt-clod fight.

Remember when my trapped tadpoles grew into forgotten frogs? You were the one I turned to with their cannibalized remains, watching in awe as you dumped them out, stone-faced, onto the dry dirt.

I knew you before Robbie Muñez pulled the head off your Barbie towards the end of fourth grade; before you punctured Barbie's head with nails and threaded it onto a rainbow-colored string. You wore that head around your neck for weeks, just to taunt Robbie—biting him when he tried to snatch it away. When he threatened to tell, you let him kiss you on the lips, twice, beneath the low branches of the playground tree.

Then one summer you budded, pushing out like a prickly pear in all the places I remained flat. When you showed up to homeroom clouded in Aqua Net and Impulse body spray, even I couldn't help whispering behind your back.

Freak.

That was the year you spit on the No Trespassing sign by the dry wash and sliced your leg on the barbed wire fence. I was too worried about getting caught to follow.

I begged you not to do it, didn't I?

Or did I bite my tongue and watch you go?

I stayed silent while you said yes to adventure, yes to ditching class, yes to the pilfered pack of Winstons from your grandfather's shirt pocket. When you offered me one, I shook my head. You smoked one after another behind the bushes—said your throat burned with the tang of asphalt and leather—while you practiced blowing smoke rings around stars in the black sky.

Someday, you swore, you'd make it out of here.

I knew you as the Sophomore with restless legs, knees juddering. When had you grown so jumpy? Remember in high school when you pulled me into the back of a car crushed with boy sweat and strawberry Boone's Farm? We hadn't spoken in months, but that night I held your hair behind the Quick Mart while you puked until you dry-heaved.

You said you'd missed hopscotch and tadpoles and me.

Said you loved me.

Begged me to stay out past curfew, your finger tracing the curve of my cheek.

When my parents grounded me for three months, I thought that would change you—that you'd be sorry—but it changed me instead. While I was holed up at home, you remained the girl who would take any dare, meet any conquest.

By the time I saw you again at Brenda Peterson's party, I hardly knew you. I felt like gagging when you came out of Brenda's older brother's room, swearing it was no big deal. Confessing that all guys taste warm, sort of acrid and a little like salt.

I lost track of you after that. I wanted to.

A few years later I wanted to tell you that you were right. I'd thought about you when I lost the nerve to say no in a dank dorm room. You flitted in and out of my mind like a moth, buzzing in my skin, beating against my heart under the faulty fluorescent light. I wanted to ask you about other things, but I swore I wouldn't look back. You hadn't, so why would I?

That's what I told myself, every time. And then time passed. A few months? Maybe a year? But when my mom sent the newspaper clipping, time stopped.

'*Woman caught in trailer fire,*' the caption read. '*A blue single-wide, twelve miles outside of town.*'

My boyfriend's hands snaked around my middle, trying to pull me back to bed.

He asked, *Who's that girl?*

And I shrugged.

I shrugged and let his hands close around me. Underneath him, I could pretend it wasn't true.

I could pretend there was still time; that there was still a chance for you and me. I could pretend you were still out there, rummaging through the charred remains. A suitcase, a sun tea jar, a child's coloring book clutched in your hands—one finger stroking the blackened edges and your eyes lifted skyward, still searching for a way out.

Catch and Release

We hear it from the neighbors, first, how Ronnie's mouth unhinges. How Ronnie is caught swallowing whisky behind the corner shop, pills outside the laundromat, and boys under the gym bleachers.

By summer, the full moon expands tight in Ronnie's belly, and I figure she must have swallowed that too. But no one confirms this, so I flounce around her wearing my swimsuit, with tanned limbs and breast buds like bottle caps, stealing glances at her moon.

Ronnie pulls the curtains closed and beaches on the sofa.

"Go!" she shouts. "Get out of my face."

But I can't look away.

Ronnie glows all summer.

In late August, we drive to the hospital.

The adults sip coffee from styrofoam cups with steeled lips. Next to his mother, the pimple-pocked boy who did it shifts this way and that in a scratchy blue chair.

I could build sandcastles from their silence.

I could build skyscrapers.

The windows grow dark and the waiting tick-tick-ticks by, fizzing my insides. Mama lets me walk-don't-run down the long hallways, and my shoes make satisfying squeaks on the gray linoleum. After thirty-nine squeaks, Ronnie screams.

Something inside me pops.

I catch her voice in my heart as her next scream rips through the green doors. Doors that say: No Unauthorized Admittance. They swing open and shut and open again, revealing images like a View-Master reel: A doctor in splattered scrubs. A tray of bloody instruments. A pink squirming baby in a see-through tub.

A nurse pushes the baby out and away.

Back in the waiting room, the adults let out their breath. The pimple-pocked boy whines, "Can we go now?" His mother nods, collects her purse, and shuffles him away.

They rustle out the door like signed paperwork.

When Ronnie comes home, she's alone. She doesn't glow anymore. She doesn't swallow anything. She's just an empty shell. A pocket of wet sand.

I know better than to press my ear against her. To listen for the rolling of the sea or touch her hand with mine.

"Get out!" she shouts.

It's the last week of summer, so I put on my swimsuit and walk to the pool.

My friend Karen is there, and we race through the blue water until we're breathless. Until Karen's sister brings out her baby and places him in Karen's arms.

Karen bounces him in the water, counting one-two-three. Prodding him to say, "Auntie, auntie, aunt."

Water splashes Karen's face, and the baby gurgles a laugh. His gums shine pink. His mouth holds a single white tooth, a sliver of shell. Milky drool slips down his chin.

I imagine my mouth unhinging, like Ronnie's, and swallowing the baby, the pool, the entire summer in one great gulp.

Ducking my head under, I swim to the deep end. The baby's squeals sound muffled from here, like a dolphin crying in the deep.

I picture Ronnie at home with the curtains closed around her.

And sinking down, I touch bottom.

Girls of Summer

1.

We go to the river, stand on the bank like true girls of summer, our bare legs exposed in bikinis as red as our mothers' lips, our long hair flowing like gypsies. We're thirteen-fourteen, brave enough to call to the boys on the other side, "Hey, lover!" like we've seen in the movies, stupid enough to dare each other to jump in.

We say we'll gasp when the cold water courses through us. We'll splash about, flail our arms, pretend to drown, white flecks of water catching the light while we wait for the boys to save us. We'll float downstream to the low bridge where we can grab onto the pillar, hoist ourselves breathless onto the bank. You'll shake out your long hair and laugh, your scarlet bikini flashing against pale skin like a warning beacon.

2.

From the water's edge, it's only a quarter mile to the low bridge. We've had years of swim lessons; our strong arms have been holding each other steady since we could stand. You check your bikini ties—a ruby red our mothers would kill us for wearing if they knew—and we dare to jump. The cold water cuts our breath, slows our legs, your hand slips out of mine, and we're begging the boys across the other side to save us.

The river rushes toward the bridge, tumbling our bodies, whipping us against the pillar like rag dolls. I claw my way to the bank. I cough until the blood beats back in my limbs. I scream your name, scream for help, stare into the water and swear I see your gypsy hair wound, weighted down. The day they find you, dusk washes the sky with cloud flecks the same pink as your cheeks.

3.

When we sneak down to the riverbank, it's early summer, and the water's coursing cold with late mountain snow melt. We're brave enough to jump, but we don't. We don't. Instead, we lay out in bikinis, kept secret from our mothers, showing off large swaths of sun-blushed skin to the boys on the opposite bank. We're stupid enough to think we have years left, to dream of futures in the bright white houses across the river, naming our children, two each—girls of summer, like us.

We swear we'll let them grow their hair long as gypsies and wear whatever they want; we'll never tell them they're too young. We'll cry at their weddings and when we're old, we'll sit out on the veranda in the evenings like movie stars, sipping on martinis and laughing, making plans for tomorrow, our lipsticked mouths matched to the crimson colors that bridge across the setting sky.

From Within the Juniper

There's a space inside the juniper bush out front. Big enough for you to crawl inside and close the musky green branches over yourself. The blueish-silver balls tickle arms and legs where the green needles don't scratch. You pinch the little balls between your fingers, rub their leathery skin back and forth between thumb and first finger. Back and forth until it bruises and your fingertips turn pungent and sticky.

From within the juniper, no one sees you. No one hears if you keep real still.

The mailman drives up and opens the mailbox over your head. The flag squeaks down. Shuffle of envelopes. A scrape and ting of metal as the door closes.

Other cars whizz past on the road. Tires grip the asphalt. Tiny pebbles scatter in their wake.

Jimmy from down the street rides by on his bicycle making weird boy noises—*braaaah broooon bruuhnn*—and practicing wheelies. Up and down. Up and down. He wrecks near your bush. If you reached out your hand, you could touch his front tire. Scare the life out of him. Make him mad.

Instead, you hold your breath, just in case. But he gets up and rides away. He doesn't see you. No one does. Not even when the sky purples and the cars begin to wink their headlights like they're sending a secret message. You try to read it through the feathery needles. Because maybe it's a message from your sister, a message from heaven, from the great beyond. Maybe she's telling you something. Maybe, if you sit here long enough, she'll come and find you, just like she used to.

A Baby Born En Caul Can Never Drown

1.

En caul babies are as rare as giant squid and underwater cairns. En caul means born inside the amniotic sac, a mermaid birth. En caul babies are the luckiest humans on earth.

When you're old enough to read, you find such facts in books.

You repeat these facts as a mantra, the forced breath tickling your skin, forming a protective bubble around you each time your mother's shifting moods wrap your ears in darkness.

Lucky.

With this word you pinch yourself clean.

2.

Your mother doesn't believe in luck.

When you were born, early in the bath, she refused to hold you. One look at your membranous face, your slick features exaggerated in the blood-skin bubble of jelly water, and your mother pronounced you defective, deformed. A black-lagoonal creature. A blue-gilled monster.

She says she didn't feed you for five long days, not until your howling pierced the milk from her breasts with the weight of a steel anchor. For months she had wished you away with scalding water, gin, and emmenagoguial herbs. But you were stubborn.

On the blackest nights, your mother recounts your flailing limbs, purpling against the white porcelain bath, the pinking water. Her terror. On those nights, she still wishes you were never born.

Lucky, you say. *Lucky*.

3.

Every winter, Mother takes you to the sea where shrilling gulls dip under seal-gray clouds along the shoreline. She waves you away from the dancing foam, the slick algal stones, the deep drop. She flicks cigarette ash windward and her warning mingles with the slow exhale of smoke.

"Don't fall to your death. Not today. I have other plans."

You hear what you want to hear. You hear, *Don't die*. You hear love prickling at the edges.

The salt spray scatters upwards, soaking your face, leaching through your light blue dress and the loose tips of your thistled hair.

4.

When you are ten, the tenuous line between mother and daughter softens and swells.

Your mother is in love.

Lightness plays at the sides of her face the way sunlight glances off the sea. These flashes of hope sustain you like an umbilical tether. You let yourself dream of a father, a picture-book pink house with wide-windowed eyes, and the three of you stretching hand in hand under a sun-smiled sky. You try to tie yourself to this image, but the winter storms wash it free.

5.

Your mother makes more attempts at love. At men.

Now you are thirteen, a miniature adornment of her with newly perked breasts and angled hips. *Lucky*. Lucky to be so like her.

But at your shifting shape, your mother comes untethered. The darkness takes her in waves, and you're sure you must be at sea, the ground below ever-moving.

She far corners you, pushes you away—but without a mother, every girl is an island. So you suction yourself. Grip on. Grip to hope. Weave plaits of seaweed and starfish into your hair, try to be more beautiful. When that doesn't work, you make yourself ugly—fish bladder eyes, sand-pocked skin—so she won't see you as competition. So she'll bat her eyes with pity, reel you in again, really look at you this time, consider where you might fit in, consider *you*.

6.

When the gloam washes the sky red-gold, you walk to the sea. You want her to notice that you've gone. To catch you at the black-slipped rocks and say, *Not today.*

Gulls shroud the air.

You dip your toes sandward, searching over your shoulder for her familiar form, her swinging gait. You imagine her running, calling out. But the path behind you smooths into shadow.

She's not coming.

The truth thunders through you, muddies your mind like an algal bloom. You think of the men, gone, all gone. Her wailing pitch loosening the hinges, chasing after them.

You'll show her. You'll hide. Worry her. Bury yourself under the sand. Crash yourself under the waves, wait for her to come. To seek, to find. For your absence to weight her heart, to grow new strings.

The icy water licks at your legs, your chest, but you wade further. Sinking into the deep, under the rising bottle-green light, you clam yourself in until your steam dissipates. Your frothed bubbles become prayers. Promises. Tessellated signals.

Are you looking? Here I am. Here.

Each utterance rises in small moons, tiny eggs of hope. You want them to pinch your mother clean.

Lucky, you say, *lucky*.

Rare as giant squid, en caul babies never drown.

With your mantra you construct underwater cairns. You wait for each word to fracture the surface, pop the sound, wing their way to your mother's ears, nestle into her soft center and set anchor.

Heart-Tongue Connection

My daughter's imaginary friend has an invisible seeing-eye dog.

At each meal, Lottie insists I fix a plate for her fake friend and another dish for the fake dog—who, unlike Lottie, is starving.

We haven't had a real dog in this house for ten years, not since before Lottie was born. But when her dad moved out six months ago, he bought one for his no-longer secret family. We spy the dog in a photo Christmas card—a retriever topped with red antlers—trapped between her dad's other children, a boy and a girl in matching green sweaters.

A seeing-eye dog, Lottie brags, is far superior to any 'reindeer' dog. It can see inside of people and sense danger. Every bark is a warning, and, according to Lottie, the invisible seeing-eye dog barks nonstop.

Because a special dog needs a special diet, I allow Lottie to concoct the most ludicrous combinations: Marmite with bananas, pimento olives in oatmeal, ketchup on custard. Tonight, at Lottie's insistence, the fake dog is having two hard-boiled eggs with jam.

I boil the eggs with a splash of vinegar to increase peelability, and when they've cooled, Lottie helps me prepare them. We smack them on the counter edge, roll them under our palms until the shells look like crackle paint, and slip the peels off.

"Now, we squeeze them between our fingers," Lottie says.

"Like this?" I ask, but I know it's right. It's how I felt when her dad left.

We squish the eggs until the remains are a sulfury mash, and that's when she stirs in the jam. A whole jar of blackcurrant—her dad's favorite, left behind too. Lottie takes the spoon, swirls the mixture round and round, and—as her dad would have done over any meal—adds five twists of black pepper.

"Don't—" I start to say but choke the words back.

Instead, I take a peppery pinch and put it on my tongue like I remember seeing my mother do. I hold it there until the spark of heat fades, until my eyes stop watering, until the memory of my mother's voice reminds me of the heart-tongue connection. How the tip of the tongue tells the state of the heart. And in order to heal the heart, my mother used to say, you go through its child—the stomach.

I run my fingers through Lottie's long, dulling hair and ask, "Lottie, darling, are you hungry?"

Lottie winces, shrugging herself away from my touch, then covers her ears.

She insists the seeing-eye dog is starving, and could I hurry up? The fake dog circles my legs, barking, until I place its dinner on the floor. Then I prepare separate plates for Lottie, her imaginary friend, and me.

Lottie spends most of the meal helping the imaginary friend locate her knife and fork. She feigns surprise when her friend scatters peas across the table and snorts when the peas roll onto the floor.

Like a good mother, I beg Lottie to take bites. I count each forkful of potato that dissolves on her tongue. It's not enough. How can I heal her, the way my mother would heal me, if Lottie swears she isn't hungry?

Instead of eating, Lottie throws her head back in fake laughter. She explains her imaginary friend's inside jokes about wingless birds and drowning mermaids; jokes that make as much sense as a secret wife and secret children. Laughter that sounds as hollow as a secret family stowed away in a secret neighborhood—one her dad had previously proclaimed too rich for people like us. Too rich, like the dog's dinner of blackcurrant eggs by the back door.

Now, after she tires of laughing, Lottie cries that her imaginary friend hasn't eaten. Lottie pretends to look away while I stab at the friend's steak and pile her potatoes onto my own.

I clear my plate; swallow to bursting, and Lottie turns her eyes to the dog's bowl.

The seeing-eye dog hasn't eaten either, and I know what Lottie wants me to do.

I bring the bowl to the table and scoop the purple-black paste onto my plate, grimacing when I take the first bite. Lottie watches, her mouth opening like a goldfish, in sync with mine. And I pass her the spoon.

Mother Tongues

I can't afford a dress for the dance, so when I win one in a raffle, my mother is thrilled. It's not the best dress; it's hideous pink and frilled-lizard ugly. It has a stiff Victorian-lace collar and the neckline bears a petalled row of pink tongues, thick as craft foam, long as lady's fingers. Another spray of tongues adorns the bustle above my ass.

The tongues dart about wildly, licking at my neck in the most irritating way.

It's exactly the kind of dress you'd expect from a giveaway, and though I'm no Molly Ringwald, I think I can work with it. But because I'm thirteen or fifteen, my mother makes the rules. When I pull and scratch at the tongues, my mother slaps my hands and gives me a lashing.

She drags hard on her cigarette, creases puckering the skin around her lips, and says, "Do NOT alter this dress. It's perfect!"

Her stiff smile holds me in a spotlight. I can't tell if she thinks this dress is the height of fashion or if she's trolling me, as competitive mothers do.

So I do nothing.

I do nothing for years.

By the time I get to the dance, I'm a mother myself, and the tongues are tired of waiting.

The tongues lick red weeping welts up my neck and clear across my chest. I fail to still my scratching hands and a tongue breaks off, wriggling in my fingers, straining wet inside my fist.

I pace the outer corridor of the dance hall, a wide white-bricked circle, looking for a safe place to toss the tongue and spy my daughter with her boyfriend.

My daughter doesn't ask for permission. She doesn't ask what's wrong. She just says, "How can we help?"

They follow me to the restroom. It smells like a locker room after a home game—part popcorn, part sweat, part piss. The sticky floors pull at the soles of my shoes, and I toss the loose tongue in a corner. It darts through a puddle, flicking and flashing, flailing itself against the dingy wall and disappearing into a pile of dirty tissues.

Under the fluorescent lights, my daughter gasps at the rash and starts attacking the tongues. She twists, tugs, and rips. Her boyfriend tries to help, but somehow he latches onto my bra instead, pulling and stretching the beige band like taffy. When I correct him, he laughs, and underneath the immaturity I sense an attempt toward helpfulness that he'll grow into.

Together, we destroy the wagging tongues, shred the lace frill, and tip them in the large painted trash barrel where, like headless fish, they give one last dying twitch.

"Wait," my daughter says, plucking the last tongue above my ass. "That's better."

Patches of hot glue remain, dotted in tell-tale globules around the neckline, but I don't care anymore. Not about my mother's rules. Not about what she says, nor what others think. Let them talk.

Already the music has started. It thumps under the door crack, vibrates through the bricks. And though I'm no longer thirteen or fifteen, I'm ready. I will dance all night under that disco ball—the hideous pink fabric swishing, flashing like Lite-Brite plastic around me.

How to Knit a Better Mother

Materials:

100% natural fibers for natural warmth, in recommended shades on circular needles.

Feet:

Cast on, starting with the soles, to help her recognize the importance of a firm foundation. Take care to get the arches just right so that she doesn't mind pacing the hallway when you have colic, walking you to school, or waiting for you at the bus stop. Knit sturdy footwear in a garish shade of honesty, so she won't lie and say no one will ever notice your shoes.

Legs:

Use coarse wool in a strong herringbone stitch to create muscular calves. Take care not to craft them too shapely nor too fine, so she won't be tempted to show them off at parent-teacher conferences, school plays, or when your dad's boss comes to dinner. Make her thighs full and her ass large—not so large the kids in the neighborhood refer to her as "Fat Ass," but large enough that it doesn't fit comfortably into your own jeans.

Stuff the thighs and buttocks firmly to create a wide comfortable lap, the kind you can crawl into for story time, after Julie breaks your doll, or after another kid breaks your heart. Make her lap strong enough for at least two grandchildren at a time and soft enough that it feels like a down-filled cradle. Dress her in dark slacks so tiny fingerprints won't show.

Torso:

Switch to an elasticated ribbing pattern, both firm and forgiving, so the next forty years aren't spent blaming stretch marks on you. Continue upwards, creating average-sized breasts (stuff carefully to avoid suspicious lumps) and a strong, straight-back. Purl her spine firmly, so she doesn't waver and can stand up to both your school principal, when he calls about the twenty-three unexplained absences, and the judge who uses the refrain 'boys will be boys' as an excuse. Reinforce her spine with a steel rod.

Arms:

Knit drop stitch shoulders in a bright shade of pride and strong arms that fit perfectly around you. Measure twice to be sure. Switch to an alpaca thread for the hands, in a supportive tone, so they'll feel soft against your cheek when she wipes away your tears. Make them nimble, for scooping pills from your mouth, but too delicate to withstand slapping your face. Take care when binding off the fingertips not to let them point in accusation when you dent the front fender on the car.

Head and Neck:

Pick up stitches from the top of the torso. Create a strong neck then increase rapidly for a large oval head, big enough to house a decent-sized brain and stuff it with oxytocin. Take care not to shape the nose too high and haughty nor the chin too small. Cable the mouth into a wide, open smile, the kind that laughs at your jokes and not at your expense. Use a soft shade just right for kisses when she checks your brow for fever or says goodnight and tucks you in.

A note about tongues—Tongues can be tricky! Pick a color in the shade of compassion. Be sure to check your gauge, so it isn't too loose and spills all your business (like telling the Kroger's cashier about the car, about your virginity, about the rape), nor too tightly, so that her mouth constantly puckers in distaste. Take care to round the tip so she doesn't develop a tendency to criticize or nag, or say other things she might later regret.

Fashion her ears like Solo cups, in equal shades of willingness and non-judgment. Make them sensitive enough to sense distress but not the secrets you whisper on the phone with your friends.

Carefully select a warm color of understanding for her eyes. Don't shape them too round in surprise nor too narrow in focus, and embroider the smallest touch of water (color shade: *Humanity*) so she doesn't think it's shameful to cry.

Finishing:

Knit her a wide heart with double deep pockets, using a strong shade of empathy, so when you find the courage to tell her you're hurting, she'll hold you close and say, *Me too.*

Uncle Donny's Secret Business

My cousin Cherise arrives for the summer bookended by her parents who have secret business meetings in Europe. I kick at the door frame, wishing Cherise and her three Gucci suitcases were staying somewhere else, while Mom invites them in. Cherise is fourteen now. She's tall, like Uncle Donny, hair feathered like a yellow bird, and squishy in all the places I'm not.

Uncle Donny kisses me hello with wet lips. Takes my hands, lifts my arms away from my sides, and says I'm shaping into a real beauty. Says Dad will need to lock me up soon, once I blossom like his Cherise.

I squirm out of his grasp and catch Aunt Trina's narrowed eyes, see her lips thin into flat worms, before she follows Mom into the kitchen.

On the sofa, Cherise crosses and uncrosses her legs, jiggling first one knee then the other, like a motorized toy buzzes inside her, until Uncle Donny places his meaty hand on her thigh, his nail beds blanching against her skin. Uncle Donny rubs Cherise's thigh until redness blooms in her cheeks.

Rubs his porcine belly and laughs, head tipped back, echoing full down his throat.

It's the kind of laugh Dad calls infectious; the kind of mouth Mom says could swallow babies.

That night, after her parents leave, Cherise tucks herself into the corner bed, tightness falling from her body like an unbound braid. She parts my diary on her lap and flicks through the pages with bored slender fingers.

Perfectly round cigarette burns cut a trail up her arm, and I imagine all the i's in the world missing their dots. She closes my diary, strokes the textured cover, and asks if I've ever done it. If I ever feel pressed tissue-paper thin.

Asks if my dad's coming in to kiss us goodnight.

Women Get Hungry

I'm downstairs waiting on Bob, my right swipe, when Aunt Sharon arrives with dating advice.

"You don't think I caught three husbands by chance, do you?"

I roll my eyes and she pronounces me a gob of pith in the marmalade. "Stop skulking and show us a bit of honey."

I turn a slow circle in my navy dress and bare my teeth like a chimpanzee, like a five-year-old at the snap of a camera. She clucks, saying my teeth are too big for my face.

"You should keep your mouth shut tonight and not go blabbering on as if you know things."

"But I do know things," I remind her.

"Not on a first date, you don't. You need to be more willy warehouse, less rocket scientist. And God forbid, don't bring up climate change."

If I'm lucky, she says, he'll only look at my tits.

"It's a shame you don't fit into Angie's gold lamé halter with the side slit. Now that was a dress." Her eyes shimmer upon reflection.

"Didn't she get raped wearing that?"

Aunt Sharon cackles, hands on hips, says rape had nothing to do with the dress.

"Angie had heels like a hooker." She spreads her thumb and forefinger into a wide curve. "I told her no good would come of shoes like that."

"Because she couldn't run?"

"Angie ordered the sirloin *and* the fish!" she cries. "In those heels. What was he to think?"

She raises her penciled brow like a punchline.

Angie. How her laugh used to vibrate from her belly and fill the room.

"Women get hungry?" I offer.

"Exactly," she says. As if everything is illuminated.

Babe Talk

"Babe," my brother says. "*Babe*."

I'm hiding in the hallway, taking notes—trying to learn more about love—while my brother's on the phone with his girlfriend Barbara. Aka Barbie-warbie, aka Booboo-doll, aka *barf*.

I like *his* Barbara, but the gooey name thing is beyond me.

"Babe," he says, pulling the cream phone cord taut, the coils uncoiled, reduced to undulant waves. Undulant—a word I learned from his Barbara.

"Babe, I love only you. Babe—*Baaabe*," he repeats like an incantation. "Babe, I swear I didn't cheat!"

Barbara's wailing slips through the phone holes, swelling in the air. My brother holds the receiver out from his ear and grimaces. Barbara sounds like a whale or a bludgeoned bear, her dying cry amplified as if echoing inside a cave.

"Babe," he tries again, his crooning gentler this time, soft as a ginger kitten's belly. Soft as that time we found a beagle bleeding in the road. Broken leg, bruised paw. *It's okay, babe*, he'd whispered. *We better get you to a vet.*

Poor Barbie-warbie doesn't get a vet though, does she?

Bleeding. That's how I imagine her, his Barbara, broken on the road. My brother behind the wheel, engine revving—BAM!

Is that what love feels like? Like any minute you're on the street, headlights stunning, caught unaware?

I shouldn't like to fall in love, if that's the case. If—like Barbara with the bouncy boobs and the big words (who is nice and all even if she does look like a lizard with teeth)—some boy is going to crash through my life and leave me broken. Busted.

"Babe," my brother says again, soft as bunny ears and granny elbows. Breathy enough to make any girl swoon.

I wonder if it's working, if he'll win her back. If this other girl—the one she spied him with at World Skate, wheels locked in a dark corner—was worth it. If by saying 'babe' enough times, Barbara will forgive him.

My brother's voice is butter slick. Even I feel myself bending to his side, brushing off his transgressions. Could he use this babe talk on Mom when he's late for curfew? *Babe* to Dad when he wants to borrow the car? Babe to his teachers, to his someday boss?

Is there a limit to what *babe* can achieve? To what *babe* can make better?

My brother, the great orator backlit behind a podium, *babe*-ing all over the Gettysburg Address. *Babe*, he says, and heals the nation. *Babe* to the terrorists and hostage holders. *Babe* for nuclear disarmament and to quell unrest in the Middle East. *Babe*—soothing astronauts stuck in space; *Babe, this is Mission Control, can you read me? Can you read me, Babe?*

Barbara's sobbing has grown softer now, and I can sense him closing in.

"Babe," my brother croons through the phone with enough conviction to cure cancer.

"Babe," like he's pleading his case to St Peter.

"Babe," greasing the hinges on his Barbara's pearly gates.

Ewe

You find it while walking the dog with Warren, watching evening shadows on asphalt lengthen between you, waiting for the dog to shit; waiting for him to circle round, nose to the ground. The dog knows the right place by sniff, the way you thought you'd know by pheromones, that the right man would just smell right, and yet—that's when you happen upon the sheep, ripped wide open, blood-soaked wool with entrails trailing.

Before you, a small mass in the center of the path—*Is that a...?*

Yes, a heart, Warren says, as if he finds one every day.

You think of your mother, how apropos she would have said, chuckling over brunch with her friends, as if your failing love life was a punchline, as if you hadn't grown up knowing acutely the sensation of your heart laid bare, cut out, until you met Warren.

This time was supposed to be different. This time, you thought you knew by taste, by texture, by the vibration in the air that swept under your skin and surrounded you both in an aura of pink light. You swear you believe in science, but the air used to vibrate pink, that is, smell like a new home before the dog, before the long hours at work, before the sip of time folding in on itself.

Maybe it's thieves, Warren says, *gutting sheep for the fun of it*, and you think of your mother again, ex-boyfriends one through seven, though three was the worst and left visible wounds; it's then that the heart lifts a little, moves, you swear. You pull the dog's collar, tell him to leave it, but Warren pokes it with a stick.

Don't, you say, remembering you heard once that the human heart is the size of a fist, and if so, this sheep's heart could be your heart, the same, red-smooth and weeping, the aorta still attached, and you want to break the stick and ask him, *Do you still love me?*

But you don't want to be that kind of woman—desperate, uncertain, nagging—the kind who plans it out like a blueprint: years of dating, months of engagement, wedding favors embroidered with a spray of flowers and invitations embossed in gold, fractions of children, checkboxes and scoreboards and honey do lists—everything perfectly chambered, each task a synchronous valve that opens and lets in a little more air, a little more life, a steady rhythm.

It's still moving, Warren says, and opens his pocketknife. He makes a clean incision and pries cardiac muscle, atria, ventricles, Valentines, true love, until the vibrating bloody chamber opens, and whatever was inside slips free.

Why an Ambulance Was Called to The Roadhouse on 17th Street After I Had Flown

Daryl calls his ex-girlfriends cuckoos, tells me they are crazy with a capital C. He shakes his head when he talks about them, tells me he must have been insane to chase birds like those.

On our first date, he brushes the hair from my face with featherlight fingertips and stares so deep into my eyes he swears he sees our future there—four kids, a house on the lake, a weekend getaway in the Greek isles.

Daryl's lips linger on my cheek, hover hot on my ear.

Cuckoos. But not you, Daryl says, using his tongue to trace our lifetime down the life line on my palm. Showing me the crease where my heart line changes, where I'll have a choice.

One day, he says, *I'm going to ask you.*

We end up fucking on the first date and every day after, for two weeks, before he ghosts me.

I park outside his place of work, watch him through the window. Three cars behind, I trail him to the bar, spy his fluttering fingers in another woman's hair, outlining her cheek, telling her about me.

Cuckoo, he says, drink catching in the back of his throat.

Osmosis

The guy who wants to date my daughter shows up an hour late, swings his long hair like a cape and brings my daughter a square bottle of whisky with fruit in it, not flowers or an apology for being late but whisky and yes, I roll my eyes even though I'm nearly forty and my mother—oh, that bag, she's delighted that my nineteen-year-old look-a-like daughter has finally attracted some male attention because God knows we aren't designed to get through this life alone—that bag beams like Cape Boy has brought my daughter an island or her own Fortune 500 company and I know that look, it's the very same look my mother gave both Bobby McCleary from the eighth grade science fair and Tony Beckley from the Bright Street Baptist Church social, saying why can't you date a boy like that, though I was only thirteen and then sixteen and twenty years later she still doesn't understand the difference between organic chemistry and sexual chemistry, how basic Tony was and caustic at that and I was practically a lemon—let's face it, I'll always be a lemon—and too small to have had any hope of neutralizing Tony Beckley when he set his mind to something, how my words and my weight weren't enough, how Cape Boy's hair and his whisky aren't enough; so what if I roll my eyes, if my mother says I'm overreacting, never mind that he's late and the whisky is homemade in a clear square bottle and my daughter, who is still young enough that I remember the weight of her in my hands after she slid out onto the bedsheets just before dawn and didn't cry, didn't even so much as gurgle, even when the midwife held her face down and rubbed her sticky back and suctioned and suctioned the fluids out of her while I held my breath but forgot to pray as if me holding mine would make her finally breathe, my daughter though she's legally an adult still barely weighs more than a pencil and doesn't know how the fruit gets saturated, that it's simple osmosis, and if you're a pencil-sized girl you might not factor the equation and think it's just fruit Mom it's just one piece and then two and a sip and it doesn't seem like actually drinking because no one does math in the moment, imagines waking up in a dark room without pants and a Grand Canyon-sized ache and for all you know you could still be in Arizona but maybe not, and maybe just maybe you're in some shack in Nevada on a brown-stained mattress with no sheets and the curtains drawn tight in occlusion, and who brings whisky on the first date anyway unless they have one thing on their mind, like Tony Beckley and those boys hiding Everclear in fruit punch and chucking slices of oranges in because they knew we wouldn't drink beer and liquor is quicker in a ruby elixir and would get us good and goosey loosey so they could hide other things inside us, so deep that even when they finished a bit of them remained—and this guy, this fucking wavy-haired late but he brings whisky guy!—if they just wanted to have sex they could have asked should have asked, instead of leaving us wondering why our mothers hadn't warned us about alcohol and boys and the damned fruit in and their stupid short hair, wavy hair, hair that flows like a cape instead of telling us we were overreacting, like now, like when he shows up an hour late for a date with the damned whisky and my mother has that look in her eye that says nobody stays pencil-thin forever and if you're alone in this world you're nothing you're nothing you're nobody you're sure you don't want to have a taste, he came all this way, despite her I turn to my daughter and say: do the math, it doesn't take much, and warn and plead with the memory of every caustic Tony and every girl with her soft permeable heart and every mother that could have said should have said something, and say: it can sneak up on you, baby girl, and fuck this guy and his whisky with fruit in, and say: I need to you to keep breathing.

Marsupium

Heading home from the hospital, I climb into the front seat of the car, next to you, and nestle the tiny baby in my lap—a baby as pink and helpless as a hairless pup, as underdeveloped as a newborn joey.

We hadn't been pregnant long—not long enough, note the doctors—before the baby slipped into our world as suddenly as a summer thunderstorm, all embryonic-webbed limbs and paper-thin eyelids.

To say we're unprepared is an understatement.

We don't yet own a baby seat, and it's not safe sitting up here unprotected—I know this—and yet there's no other choice. I strap the baby in with me; imagine us crashing, my body folding on top of hers like a tin can, crushing her.

Her too small body disappears behind the seat belt.

You remind me that newborn kangaroos are no larger than a grape. And unless I'm a marsupial, there's nothing else we can do.

So we drive on.

We drive through dingy gray airport terminals, cream-coated malls—long hallways that turn and twist like labyrinthine canals. Shops stretch up on both sides. Suitcases, baby bottles, bassinets hang from racks and rafters. I crane my eyes, cradle the baby pouched in my lap like precious cargo, and point my voice at the stores that might sell baby seats. But there's nowhere to park, no way to stop.

So we drive on.

Roads widen into byways and highways, dizzying our eyes with headlights and glowing green road signs, until the blacktop creeps into the color of the sky.

Finally, we find a shop with parking, but the vibe is all wrong. A neon sign fizzes from a restaurant across the street. Graffiti menaces from the shop's outer walls, and whining fluorescent lights jaundice the shop's insides.

I wander the cramped aisles, baby cupped to my stomach, eyes trailing over the offerings, everything a thousand sizes too large. I meet the manager's eyes and recognize my mistake echoed back at me like a bullet.

They don't make seats this small for a reason.

I hug the tiny baby tighter into my pouched stomach and head back to the car, to you, but find myself lost in the parking lot where everyone's on high-alert. There's a deep-earth hum and a throng of terror-twisted faces, hair on end on end.

Predators.

Across the lot, a squelching dark puddle.

Blood inside the shop. Blood outside. The smell like copper wire. The shine of the surface. The heft.

I have a baby, I beg. *Please.*

From faraway, I hear myself keening. The baby burrows into my sagging stomach and my skin softens around it.

To say we're unprepared is an understatement.

You catch my hand and remind me that marsupials, when threatened, sacrifice their young. Their muscled pouches open and drop the baby in self-preservation.

Ensuring their own survival allows marsupials to try again.

I climb into the front seat of the car, alone, next to you, and you buckle the seatbelt around me. We drive back the way we came—past the neon fizz, the cream tunnels. Suitcases, baby bottles, and bassinets menace in our peripheral, from racks and rafters, from roads upon roads, closing in.

Finders Keepers

You're on your way to work when you find a baby sitting on the compost heap, still damp with morning dew as if newly spawned from a forgotten seed. Fine wisps of hair sprout from its pink pearlescent head. As you pass by, its eyes pool and it whimpers—a puncturing sound that somehow seems to grow louder with each distant step.

"I'm late for a meeting," you scold the baby, knowing full well you can't leave it here. The baby gurgles while you swaddle it in leaf litter and locate a long piece of old twine. You hoist the baby, strap it to your back, and set off.

The baby, unimpressed by benchmarks and risk assessments, cries during the meeting. The fury of its gaping mouth is met by a room full of rolled eyes and wrinkled lips. You shush the baby; hand it your watch to pass the time. The baby wets the watch with slobber, slips it into its cavernous craw, and devours the watch in one great gulp. When the wailing starts up again, you jiggle the baby—first on one hip, then the other. The baby's mouth puckers at your purse strings, slurps up your credit cards and belches out long white reels of receipts.

You rock the baby, change the baby; take it outside for fresh air where strangers stop to admire the baby. They coo like pigeons and question your sanity. They say the baby is underdressed, overdressed, or depressed. They quote Kahlil Gibran's *The Prophet* and say the baby doesn't belong to you.

"If not to me, then to whom?" you ask, offering to hand over the baby. But razor-wire rises unbidden on the strangers' backs. Clutching their own watches, they retreat.

You carry the baby, and carry the baby, and like the story of St. Christopher carrying the Christ child, the baby seems to grow heavier with each step. Your very bones weep.

"Are you God?" you ask the baby.

The baby smiles beatifically, folding its wise eyes into slits, before it spits up a list of demands, drawn in crayon, all caps, on long sheets of snow. You feed it books and hand-knit sweaters, pep talks and vaccines.

When the baby coughs, you measure your youth in medicinal, syrupy spoonfuls. When it's teary, you weave a blanket from the pink striated fibers of your heart. The baby outgrows the sweaters, its arms and legs shooting out and up like runner beans. No longer toddling but towering, the baby devours the books, the television, the refrigerator—each one slipping effortlessly down its neck like a snake—and takes up smoking. Smoking!

The baby takes everything now. Takes a job, takes a lover, takes secateurs and severs the twine—the sharp snip of the steel blades sends the edges unraveling. The baby flips to the last page on your calendar. It takes one solid, sure-footed step into the square marked tomorrow and—

"Wait!" you cry.

You knot one end of the fraying mud-brown twine and put it where your heart used to be. The other end you hand to the baby, just in case.

Public Transportation

When the hippopotamus boards the crowded bus, a collective groan goes up. Bodies recoil as he sloshes down the aisle on stumpy brown legs. I place my knitting bag on the seat next to me and take out my project, praying he'll move on, but he doesn't. He stops next to my row and hovers with sulfury grunts that reek of expectation.

This is why I hate public transportation.

I huff, move my bag onto my lap, and tug my scarf higher into a makeshift respirator.

The hippo piles onto the seat like an overstuffed duvet—doesn't even say thanks—so I have to squeeze over. I want to hold my ground, but I don't want any of *that* touching me. I can't risk it; if I show up smelling like hippo, my daughter-in-law won't let me hold the baby. I know how she is.

The other women on the bus flare their eyes in sympathy.

At the next stop, three seats empty out, and I try telepathy to get the hippo to move. It's not the kind of thing you say aloud, not to a hippo. Who knows what will happen if I make him angry? He doesn't budge, and I'm left to simmer in the fog of his musk. I retreat further against the window, and the hippo relaxes into the space like a fart.

I focus my attention back to the knitting balanced on my lap—duck booties for my granddaughter. The hippo's funk might absorb into the soft yellow fibers, but the needles are sharp. If he spreads another inch, I'll poke him.

Carefully, I draw the yarn through the next round of stitches and try to concentrate. It's a difficult pattern—one I hope will score me extra grandparent points—but a familiar pang rises up. I worry my daughter-in-law won't accept me. I worry I've done the webbing wrong.

I worry and examine the directions again. The bus careens, sending the hippo toppling into me. Sending booties and needles flying. Sending my yellow yarn unspooling over the hippo's lap like Chinese noodles.

The women on the bus gasp, but no one moves to help.

Several stitches have slipped off the needle. The hippo snatches the bootie up in his thick, soiled feet. I suck in my breath, knowing exactly what my daughter-in-law would think, as he turns it over and around like a dead thing.

"Duck feet?" he asks.

"Booties," I say. "For my granddaughter." I show him my only picture of the baby, pristine and tightly wrapped in a sterile pink sheet.

"I thought if I knit something different, something difficult, they'd let me... participate."

The hippo nods, and his eyes brim like water glasses.

"She's a lucky baby," he says. And smooth as a knife through soft cheese, he slips the stitches back onto the needle and places the knitting in my hands.

Sometimes Mommy Tigers Get Sick

To suspend time, I take my tiger to the park.

I push the tiger on the swings, and he roars. He kicks his orange paws, leaps away, and launches himself down the slide. He shouts, "Catch me this time, Daddy." My tiger climbs the jungle gym and pretends it's a castle, a spaceship, our own private passageway to a forest in Asia.

Sometimes he pretends I'm a tiger too.

When he snaps his teeth at other children and I say, "Be nice, Charlie," he growls.

His little lip curls like Elvis, and I see his life flash out before him. Charlie as a ten-year-old, ripping the knees out of every pair of jeans. Charlie at a gangly fourteen with the first hint of dark hair above his lip and squeezing fat pimples in the mirror. Charlie kissing other tigers—girls or boys—learning to love, to parallel park, to bury the seeds of devastation over and over again.

Will he remember this is when it started? Look back and know this as the day he learned the bottom drops out and no one can catch him, not really?

Will he remember how I carried his tiger-pajamaed body to the playground, hair disheveled, the crusts of sleep still clinging to his eyelashes, a box of cereal clutched in his arms? How we sat by the playground—him munching handfuls of sticky loops, licking the crumbs from his paws; me, saying, "This way, tiger," as we crawled through the jungle gym, palms pushing through sand, resting our foreheads against the cool metal bars, stretching his childhood out one more day. Making it last. Making believe I was a daddy tiger who had slept the night through. Not a human dad, a husband home from the hospital, flatline still ringing his ears, struggling to say such unbearable words.

Will he remember how the sun arced above us until the streetlights clicked on, how the playground emptied out, how his tiny body slumped against my shoulder lulled by the sound of cicadas? How I stalled and said, "Let's sleep out here in the tall grass," and he forgot to growl, saying, "I want to go home; I want Mommy."

How on the long walk home, my footfall slow-slow-slow, I held him tight against my chest and listened to his heart beat a pulsing rhyme between us—my heart, slipping silently through the cracks—when I tell him.

Among the Weeds

I'm crying in my car on the side of the highway when a small boy approaches holding a pair of red rusted scissors. He has teeth like a baby shark and freckles glitter his nose.

The boy taps my window with the scissors and shouts, "You okay, lady?"

He can't be older than six. I'm parked on the soft shoulder. There are no other cars here—there's nothing for miles—so where'd this kid come from?

I gulp air, wipe my eyes and wind down the window. "Where are your parents?"

He shrugs. With two hands he wrestles the rusty scissors open and shut, scraping the blades together, and asks, "Wanna buy some flowers?"

He points to an overgrowth of tall weeds at the edge of the road.

I only have five bucks and a few butterscotch candies. I should be back in my apartment—packing, pressing my black dress and booking a flight home. Standing at the foot of my father's grave, apologizing for not being the son he wanted, instead of here on the side of the highway in the hot sun.

But the kid smiles. In his too-small t-shirt his ribcage protrudes like the breast of a bird. Hope clings to his baby shark teeth and to his eyes, half-scrunched against the light.

I can't leave him alone out here, so I get out of the car and follow him. Down the shoulder, up onto the verge, past the discarded fast-food wrappers, Starbucks cups, and what looks like—but I hope isn't—a used condom.

The high weeds tickle. Grasshoppers bounce off my shins while the boy struggles with the scissors.

"Can you help me?" he asks.

I take the heavy scissors and with both hands the boy bunches together goldenrod and seeding grasses.

"Cut 'em here," he says.

The dull blades barely chew at the stems, and I wonder when this boy last ate.

Instead, I ask, "What are you going to do with the money?"

"Make my dad happy again." The boy shrugs like it's no big thing while his eyes flick to the road and fill with shadows.

"I used to garden with my dad," I tell him. "Dahlias, carrots, potatoes—everything had to be in measured straight lines."

"He ever whip you?" the boy asks.

"Yeah," I say. "Yours?"

The boy nods, and I saw hard with the scissor-edge. The stems come away shredded, but the boy hugs the bouquet to his chest anyway and grins.

It reflects yellow on his chin.

"You like butter." I say it as if I'm still seven, playing a schoolyard game with buttercups, and the boy giggles.

All at once I want to scoop him up. Buckle him into the backseat of my car and speed home. Bathe him, feed him, tuck him under a blanket with a picture book and a stuffed bear, instead of these scissors.

In the morning, I'd buy him a box of sugared cereal with a surprise inside. Give him a spade and a spot of earth, a packet of seeds. Real flowers that he could sprinkle any which way he liked.

I could phone my mother then. Say the Disappointment isn't coming. Send this boy's flowers in my stead—goldenrods, weeds. Not have to be there when her face inevitably falls like wet plaster.

"Where's your dad now?" I ask.

The boy tells me all about his dad's rattling white truck. How he's sure to come back when he's done being angry.

Even though it's cliché, I offer the candy from my pocket. The boy doesn't seem to have been taught Stranger Danger. He takes a honeyed orb and holds it up to the sun, holds it against the golden flower heads and smiles—it's a perfect match. He sucks the candy and it balls into a hard lump in the pouch of his cheek.

Somehow, I sense the edge of it in my stomach.

I check my watch and crouch among the weeds, next to the boy. He tosses tiny pebbles and giggles when the grasshoppers jump, while I squeeze the scissors open and shut. With each metallic scrape, specks of rust flake off the blades and blow like sparks, beyond us, out into the empty road.

Each Breath a Chain

After school and on Saturdays we couple up and make-out under the overpass in the middle of town—under shirts, over jeans. Our parents say the tunnels are full of rats. They tell us to take the long way round, warn us about gang violence and drugs, but we laugh them off.

The only rat in the tunnels is Tommy, pilfering smokes from his dad's dresser drawer; so after we tire of exploring each other's contours, we can practice blowing smoke rings, each breath a link, a chain—our futures mere specks in the distance, spread out like blacktop, unbroken.

When the end of senior year approaches, Tommy dares us to camp out. We haul our sleeping bags into the tunnels, burrow into each other's warm crevices, spray paint our names and '4-ever' inside hearts. We swear by pinkies, by blood. Promise to call, to write. Say we won't change, we'll stay evergreen, but by autumn we've scattered.

The passing years scar us. We seed ourselves in new pacts, birth new promises, raise our kids to take the long way round. We warn them off gangs, off drugs, and stir fears of rats in dark places.

Our kids don't listen. They seek out the tunnels, come back reeking of spray paint and smoke, believing each breath a chain, swearing the future is a speck. Swearing time and love are untouchable. Swearing they're the ones who can make it last.

When the Girl on Seventh Avenue Offers You a Mango

She'll tell you it's an aphrodisiac. You'll laugh, rub it against your lips and ask, *Is this right?*

She'll giggle, and you'll nuzzle a slit right through the skin. She'll roll her eyes, but she won't stop you. Not when the juices drip from your chin onto the cracked asphalt of the marketplace. Not at the first sign of swelling.

She'll only be thinking about love and lips.

Years later, you'll tell your grandchildren about the ride to the hospital, how your tongue grew three sizes, how your heart grew four.

You'll tell them she still takes your breath away.

Being a Linda

Frank comes in from the fields, says, "You amaze me," and I'm thinking this is it—it's finally happened.

I'm his Linda.

He rubs his hands through his hair and paces in his work boots, three muddy steps toward the pale blue toaster leaking crumbs, seven muddy steps toward the white bookshelf overflowing with crockery and half-read paperbacks (*unread*, he'd argue, glass half-empty) and says, "Help me. I don't understand," which is music, literally, to my ears.

My mother said I'd never be anyone's Linda; as loved as Linda was by Paul McCartney, as worthy. And yet, all it took was three years, five dozen pigs, and four babies. In theory, we could have had our own babies, maybe a quartet of redheads to slop the pigs and sow the wheat, if Frank hadn't insisted on establishing himself first (*Farms don't grow themselves!*). So, instead, I'd picked the babies out from ChildFund (Gambia, Peru, Afghanistan, and—our newest—Harry from Haiti), and hung their pictures in matching brass frames over the mantle.

I would have sponsored more, but after the whole Protect the Pigs adoption fiasco, my therapist advised I focus on quality over quantity.

And my focus must be paying off because Frank reaches into the front pocket of his overalls and pulls out a piece of paper. A love song? *Please let it be a love song.*

But it's not. It's the back of an envelope where he's scratched a long string of numbers.

"I had a call from the bank—you sponsored an entire herd of horses from some island?"

"Near Greece," I say.

"Becky, you can't keep doing these—"

"What? Charitable acts?"

"Foolhardy, idiotic—" He crumples the envelope, balls it in his fist.

"But you said you wanted horses, and someone has to save them!"

"But why us?" he shouts. "Pigs, children, and now some fake horse scam? Jesus H. Christ and Mary in a basket."

Frank leans against the counter, shoulders rising with each controlled breath. Out the window, behind him, the low sun bathes the hills and surrounding fields in a reddish glow.

I imagine the horses there—how regal they'd look running free; sunlit manes, hoofs stamping—and soften my tone.

"Then what are we doing all this for?" I ask.

"This?"

"This life, Frank. This land. What are we making here together if not a better future?"

I say it like I imagine Linda would have said it, the way Linda put the world first, the way her selflessness inspired a movement, a song. Amazement.

He gives the toaster a shove, sending crumbs crashing—a year's worth of breakfasts, maybe more. But what are toaster crumbs when there's an entire planet to save?

Frank flares his nostrils. "What. Is. That. Smell?"

Oh god, I forgot the nut roast—which I now recall, too late, gave him indigestion last time. A blessing it's burnt, really.

"It's nothing," I say. "Why don't we go out for dinner? Some fresh air will do you good."

"Horses!" he shouts. "Horses!" As if he hasn't heard a word.

"Kefalonia Island," I whisper, though what I really want is to shout *Get a grip, Frank*, but being a Linda means being steadfast. Having heart. Patience—I'm sure of it.

Being a Linda is hard work.

I back out of the kitchen, escaping the tornado of Frank's fury, to find Harry, my six-foot Haitian surprise of a son, standing in the entryway.

"Shall I say hello to Papa now?"

"We're in the middle of something," I say. "Why don't you finish unpacking while I help him understand."

The Marriage Compatibility Challenge: Coupling in Exotic, Cramped Quarters

Fallout Shelter

Our raucous lovemaking reverberates off steel walls. It's eternally night, and when our bodies tire, we read and play cards in the afterglow, swearing we won't suffocate.

We promise we'll make it.

Lighthouse

The air is fresh; the light, automated. Without further purpose, we spend more time staring at the horizon, where sea meets sky, than at each other. Farouk fishes; I knit.

Monotony wears like a thin blanket.

Space Shuttle

Unbound by gravity, we float apart, tracking the oxygen meter, the emptiness, the bright blue marble—yearning for other voices, other hands, other futures.

Re-entry burns.

Knock Loudly and Wait

We marry in 1979, the week 'Ring My Bell' tops the radio and lifts the discotheque. It's all shimmer and flashing lights at first. Even when I cook the bird dry, there is always something fresh between us—the pop of a cork.

The fizzle.

Two kids and three stone later, I check your collars for clichés; find a number in your pocket. 'Repairman,' you say. Doorbell, dishwasher, disposal…

A broken litany lies between us.

About my bell? This old thing hasn't been rung in ages. Doorbell's still broken too. I reckon one's an easier fix than the other.

Home Improvement

Hank had got the curtain rod on offer for a fiver. The proud hunter, home with his find. He hadn't wanted to spend the extra ten quid on the larger rod. Surely not the extra twenty on cast iron with decorative ends. But was it too much to expect a rod that would hold things in place, or endure at least several seasons?

I hang the curtains and stand back, watch them sag in the middle, the weak aluminium buckling under the weight of lace and beige taffeta.

Store-bought not hand-sewn, like his mother offered, with the same tone she used when asking about future grandchildren or how I planned to dress the turkey. Lined in cream not white, as she had prescribed.

I knew the curtains weren't right when I bought them. I didn't have the confidence to pull off bright colours, nor the money for bold designer prints. Rather than stunning or elegant, as I'd fancied, I settled on nondescript and simple. Like always, I'd make do.

I tug, gently, to straighten the folds. The rod shifts further under the added strain.

"What's the problem?" Hank asks.

"Well… it's bent."

I suck in the rest, chew on my resentments. We'd been together long enough that I knew to say it once and stop. Breathe. Wait for his brain to catch and start like a dull motor.

He shrugs. "Looks fine to me."

To you. Of course it does.

We stand, not touching, in the curtain-sagging reverie. Watching the rod bend and dip.

Waiting for the snap.

She Always Loved the Circus

The first bruise, a ballooning big top across her cheek, is an accident. The second and third, nobody's fault. His mood roller-coasters, splitting her skin with funhouse effects that fade into sleepless crescents under her eyes until she finally whispers, *Enough*.

She pockets money and plots escape, but he sugars back in—he always does—smile stretched like warm taffy and upends her resolve with a carousel of promises. Forgiveness earns her torn pockets and another tiny witness to the sideshow.

Her bearings now forfeit, clown car full, he delivers a real showstopper.

The children hold her hand until the music ends.

Some Things Never Change

Someone has stolen my wife's head. I spot it on my morning jog, ten months after her death, in a neighbor's bedroom window. I'm always seeing her places, but this is different. Real. Same hair like the sun blazing through autumn leaves, same wide mouth tipped into a laugh. I smash my way through flowering hydrangeas—shouting, "Jenni!"—and press my nose against the cool glass. But she doesn't even flinch. Blink. Nothing. She stares right through me.

On Ten Bay Beach

We sit thigh-deep in sea water manufacturing memories with my father, so after the cancer finally kills him I can tell Benji, "You were his everything."

It's no lie; Dad has more patience for my infant son than he ever had for me.

Benji's skin glows porcelain against Dad's sunken chest while Dad's young wife snaps photos. She tells Benji to smile and me to smile and though the whole stupid memory thing was my idea, I just want to punch her in her chihuahua-stained teeth.

Dad's sitting right next to me, and I miss him already.

A Prayer to Chim Phượng

When the soldiers come, they sweep our village into a great pot and stir, searing our fathers in fields of fire. Minh and I hide in hooch and shadow, calling on Chim Phượng to carry us away. Praying our mothers and sisters will survive being split. Praying to be invisible.

They say a great bird, as red-feathered as Chim Phượng, stretched out its wide wings and carried our people here, setting seed in the furrows, sowing prosperity. Now the fields are planted with the blackened bones of our fathers, and our sisters die of shame. Our mothers hurl their swelling stomachs against rocks, seep themselves in poisons, tread treacherous paths along the river, but it's no use.

Ghosts slip from our mothers' centers, milk-white and howling with hunger. Our mothers squint at their fallow faces, pronouncing them ugly little things with horrible mouths. Too sharp, too narrow, too pale. We carry these creatures on our backs, suckle them with rice-water rags and overripe rambutan after our mothers turn them away.

When sleep comes, Minh and I dream of the great bird Chim Phượng and ride her into the mountains. We scoop water from a still spring and sprinkle it on the ghosts until our blood rises in their cheeks. We spin the bird's bright feathers into thread and stitch our mothers and sisters whole again. We crack golden eggs into the furrowed earth, and our fathers rise like giants. We lift the heavy stones from our mother's hearts, lift the babies from our backs and laugh.

In the morning, we forget our father's shining faces. The ghost babies are gone. We see their bodies bob like buoys on the river, sun-scorched shapes that settle in shadows on our mothers' hands and the sallow pockets under their eyes.

After our mothers rise, marching slow-footed to the muddy fields, Minh and I stretch our ears for the far-off whisper of gunfire. We crouch in the corners, sharpened sticks clenched in each fist, and call on Chim Phượng.

We pray that we could grow wings too.

Here is the Church

No one knows how the birds got in. But as we switched on the lights and fired up the machines, setting off the rat-a-tat-tatting of compressors and shearing metal, the birds all rose up at once. They screamed, black wings flailing, beating against the bright windows.

"We should shoot 'em," Frank said. He adjusted his coveralls and closed one eye against a shaft of morning light. God's light, we called it back home; how it cut a clean line and washed everything in possibility. The dark birds cast moving shadows over Frank's face while he took mock aim with steepled fingers. "Bang!"

I flinched. Told them about Dad making us shoot crows back on the farm. The powder smell that stuck to my fingers. How they dive bombed us from then on. "Took a chunk off my brother Paulie's ear."

Donny laughed that high-pitched squeak of his and slapped my arm. "Imagine you, shittin' yerself over some wittle birds."

I shrugged him off. "You see me cowering now? Nah. I seen worse since."

"Like what?" Frank wanted to know, but I shook my head.

One by one, I shut the machines down and threw open the doors. Figured maybe the birds would catch some breeze and see their way free.

We waited outside a good twenty minutes, Donny smoking through yellowed teeth and Frank, sitting in his truck, clicking through radio stations. Still those birds didn't budge. Some had roosted up on the sills and on the machines themselves. One or two circled, came within a couple feet of the door, but shied away when Donny got the broom out.

"You gonna help or what?" Donny asked.

"Nope." I leaned against the open doorway while Donny whooped and yelled, jumping up and down, waving with the broom.

"C'mon! Get!"

"They ain't cows, Donny," I said, and he flipped me off.

That's when Frank came in carrying a piece. "Screw this shit."

He cocked and took aim.

The shot exploded in my ears. Smell of the powder taking me back. Not to the farm, but after that, to the church. God's light glinting through the colored windows, confusion, and the rat-a-tat-tat worse than a hundred compressors.

I wish I could say I jumped on Frank. Held him down, wrestled the gun away from him. But I was no hero. Never was.

When Frank finished shooting, he kicked at my boot. Called me a sissy, said, "They was just birds."

But swear to God, when I peeled myself off the concrete and opened my eyes—through the wetness—all I saw were people.

The Hill We Die On

Daddy says it's every man's right to have a guru, and more's the pity if you only have one. Used to be that gurus were just for show, perfect for scaring off a snake or rattling your enemy's chain. Used to be that you had to be close enough to a man for your guru to have any effect. Nowadays, gurus can reach a thousand souls a minute.

Gurus in bedside tables. Gurus in cabinets, in closets, under beds. Gurus with hair-triggers kept in glove boxes and on a rack in your truck. Concealed gurus—strapped to your leg, your side—don't leave home without your guru.

Gurus used to mean something. If man wanted to protect his sheep, he got himself a guru. Protect his family? Guru. Eat? Guru. You knew when you saw gurus coming; when Chekov left a guru in the scene, someone would show up and start worshipping. Every time.

Now, we slip around in the aftermath of gurus. We pray to the gurus, let gurus run rampant, control our emotions and our politics, slide into the pockets of our leaders and our children's lunch bags.

We don't bother to hide them anymore; gurus litter every scene. Small ones, large ones, foreign, domestic, handheld, fully automated. Gurus slung over shoulders at the laundromat and the grocery store. Gurus propped-up in pews at First Street Baptist. Gurus ring out from every street corner and every channel on TV.

In the Land of Good and Plenty

Instead of good news, Daddy brings home boxes of Good & Plenty he's bought from the hospital vending machine. Sissy and I sit in front of the TV, chewing, getting the pink-and-white candies caught in our molars, the hard shell of sugar melting down our throats.

We shake the purple boxes like piggy banks, rattling with riches, and turn the TV dial. We watch Tweety Bird outwit the hungry tomcat, Road Runner outsmart the coyote, and Bugs Bunny escape the hunter's gun.

And we chew.

We chew the pink pills for sadness and the white ones for hope.

We click and chew through morning cartoons to the afternoon matinee. We chew to the tempo of 76 trombones. To the boy-meets-girl medley. To the happily ever after.

We turn-click through western shoot-em-ups and insurance commercials and stop when we see Sally

Struthers begging us to save babies. She shows their bellies swollen from hunger; their mud-streaked faces blistered in the bright sun.

Sally says we can buy a life for only seventy cents and we imagine trading our candy money for a baby brother or sister. We imagine brushing her dark hair while she coos. We try to imagine who she will reach for, and Sally tells us, "It's enough to make the angels cry."

Pink pills for sadness. White pills for hope.

Inside each one, the black sick of licorice. Bitter lump. Sugar. Bitter lump.

We click and chew all the way to dinner, our bodies wedged in the big brown chair listening to the pop and crackle of canned laughter. Our eyes fastened to the screen, instead of each other's faces and the empty spaces.

When Daddy finally remembers, "Little girls must eat something besides candy," he drags himself to the kitchen and cooks dinner. We creep from the brown chair to the brown table and find plates of liver, layered with slimy strings of boiled spinach and blood-red beets, still soft and cold from the jar. It's everything the TV says will make us strong.

"Please eat something," Daddy pleads. His eyes blink. His mouth opens and his throat closes over word-lumps he doesn't say.

We pick up our forks and slow-dance them across our plates, but we're not hungry.

"Think of the starving children in China," he says, threatening to mail our food. We imagine spinach and beets bulging from a manilla envelope, the squish of it in the mailman's hands—the gloop seeping through—and Daddy sighs, scraping our plates into the trash.

We slide from our chairs like ghosts, stepping over the space where Mama's shoes used to lay, and turn back to the TV.

Pink pills for sadness, white ones for hope.

We shake our boxes and chew.

When Neil Armstrong Walks on the Moon

The GIs puff like bánh bao dumplings and drink until their pockets leak. They point at the sky, echoing, *One giant leap*, fingering our necks with promises, tracing our thighs with kisses. We orbit around them and ask for payment up front, mindful we've other mouths to feed.

They launch their rockets, planting their flags inside us, and fly away.

Years later, when Thanh asks about his father, I finger the night sky. Talk about small steps and point out his likeness in the waxy face of the moon.

His name was Neil, I say.

Somehow, it feels true.

Havasu Falls

They say Jerry Pavis saw God the night he jumped into Havasu Falls, full moon igniting every droplet of water with an iridescent glow. Others say the water hummed his name, beckoning him like a thing bewitched.

Or maybe he just wanted to die.

Some people are like that, even with a wife and kids, money in the bank. The darkness calls them straight out of the light.

Every month we hike out to the falls and light a candle for him. I don't know if it helps, but his wife's hand sure feels warm in mine.

Lunar Landing

I go with Gary from Housewares up into the hills after work. There's a comet coming, the news says, and Gary's promised to show me the stars.

We share a six pack and a spread of dips, chips and cheeses—Gouda and soft Camembert—waiting for the sky to dim, the lights of the city to turn on.

Even though my breasts take up little space, Gary tells me I have a celestial body.

When I fantasized about this moment it was always with Mark from Electronics, him fawning over me like a satellite dish, tuning me to reach deep space. I suspected I wasn't really satellite material. The closest I'd ever come to making contact with alien lifeforms was selling negligees in Nightwear or with a church boy down the hill honking for Jesus.

Gary repositions his telescope, starts searching for habitable planets or some other signs of life, but the sky seems static. He fingers the constellations while I chew the edge of my thumbnail.

"Sometimes it takes a while," Gary says, focusing in on the hooded moon.

I stare upwards, squint, settle into the warmth from the beer. I imagine Mark from Electronics dressed as an astronaut, exploring uncharted territory, taking giant leaps for mankind, and I fall upwards into zero gravity. All at once, the stars flare supernova.

Gary floats back into my orbit, smile as bright as a serving platter, and wipes his chin.

Waxing After Waning

Your labia puffs red like a bonobo's. Cells and hair rip away, leaving you patchy and raw, blood blooming like roadkill. Now your outers match your inners. The technician shrugs, says your skin will toughen over time. You'll get used to it. Just like you'll get used to Cal's cold side of the bed, the sight of his unused coffee mug, the stinging silence of an empty house. Like when the children left for college, only Cal isn't here to make midday love on the sofa.

Cal hadn't minded hair down there, the natural state of things. Not like men today, your daughter warns. You try to imagine yourself as a manicured garden—Trim the hedges! Pull the weeds!—but your skin rubs and prickles inside your clothes. You shut the curtains, smooth on cool ointment, and remember to breathe. Remember Cal had said you should date, not mope around after… when he's gone.

Online, you swipe left. Right. Center in on a kind face. One that prefers cats over dogs, salad over steak, women of experience—whatever that means. But he's nice enough, you tell your daughter. He talks about his wife, her cancer, the circular nature of grief. Takes you to coffee, art galleries, dinner. Until it becomes, step-by-step, inevitable—trim the hedges, pull the weeds—the next step. Now you're dipped in glass, steeped in expectation. Each inch exposed and vulnerable like a hairless cat, a new-plucked chicken.

And everything, everything aches.

When Mary Wants a Word with God

she presses A3 on the hospital vending machine in order to leave a voicemail, insisting that Mary—as a name—is too heavy a burden for a baby who can't yet find her own hand, for a girl of four who's whipped for whispering an overheard "cocksucker" on the city bus, for a preteen boiling with breasts and pimples, pustules of rage and self-loathing—stamped NOT ENOUGH, stamped TOO MUCH, an abacus-counting of shortcomings and *thou shalts*—she is a slut when spied swaying against Gavin MacMillan at the senior dance, body fizzing hot pop rocks, trying so damn hard to be pretty, meaning perfect, quiet—a wanted goddess unexplored; meaning help the needy but don't talk to beggars, follow your open heart but keep your trim legs shut; meaning study hard earn less marry well pot roast suckle babies but never ever let's talk of breasts, just hope to be perfectly slotted into the plastic sleeve of some man's wallet, a propped-up arm candy porn star by night cum Donna Reed by day, DO NOT THINK OUTSIDE THE BOX, MARY, the Mother, Magdalene, the Bloody, of Scots, contrary, drowning in bitterness, the lights on the vending machine blinking in distress signal waves sending Bernese dogs trawling the mountainside, sniffing out survivors, the worthy—diagnosed by public approval ratings, by what was worn on a waist or festooned in the hair—as the vending machine corkscrews, Mary winds herself back from sagging with age to ground round grade A meat to Gavin Whatshisface, starlit bonfires, wine cooler confessionals, feeling fire-kissed by cherry bomb lipstick, to pimples to baby dolls to cocksucker pea mash spit out onto the bib of the world, demanding to know what kind of legacy is afforded a woman, decreeing to anyone in earshot, I don't need your permission; punching C7, praying: it's not too late.

On the Night of Miracles

Twelve thousand people see the face of Jesus, the outlines of their long-departed—perceive the weight of their hands, the scent of their skin—see birds rise up into the blackest sky like stars ascending. The news calls it a queer coincidence; the Church, a sign; governments, an insurgency.

At the station, five-year-year old Zara senses the tinkling of bells, fresh lavender, sees the driver jump from the train and disappear down the tracks. Until her dying breath, she swears there was light there—a woman's figure, the faraway echo of an orchestra, a crescendo of magic.

An Accumulation of Expectant Cloud Watchers Dream of First Snowfall

We sky gaze and ground squelch, sleep as though full-term pregnant—rainwater swollen, impatient with the drifting sameness of days, the dark waiting.

Tossing in discomfort, we turn, puddling into leaf decay.

At the barometric drop we worm to the windows, watching shaken trees silhouette before the amorphous-blown grey. We hold our breath. Press against panes. Pray hands to the bird-dotted delirium.

And the sky sheds!

A shush.

We are delivered. Crisped. Iced in hope.

Squinting, icicle-eyed, we step out into the miraculous *this*—joy remade!—sinking first footfall into the white-felted foam crunch.

Holy Jesus, There's a Nun in IKEA

At first I think she's a mannequin perched on an Ektorp sofa; some hipster's idea of a humorous gag in the showroom. But then she moves. Her dark veil swishes like the flash of a crow's wing as she turns to caress a shaggy silver pillow.

Matty's waiting in the car, and I'm supposed to be quick—in and out—to pick up a replacement picture frame after our wedding portrait crashed off the wall. But I can't take my eyes off this nun.

She stands, smooths out her tunic and strides past me, past the paper measuring strips and doll-sized pencils, past the cage of yellow shopping bags, and heads straight for the display of throws. She strokes each one, knit in vibrant golds and grays, and presses them against her cheek like one would a kitten.

She sees me staring and smiles. I turn away and pretend to examine an armchair, one of those wide ones big enough for two, the kind Matty says are wholly impractical. He'd have found the frame and made it to self-checkout by now, but I like to linger. Imagine what if. Stand in each decorator room and pretend to be living some alternate version of my life—a young twenty-something with a new apartment; a scientist who collects jazz records; single and on a first date, wondering if I'm brave enough to smoke a little weed if he asks, if he'll tip me over the edge of the armchair or if he'll go slow.

I should hurry, get in and out, like Matty said. But the nun's on the move, and I snake after her; I can't help myself. Her tunic swings with each graceful step, as if with every movement she gives more of herself to God. And she's beautiful, even with her hair hidden within the wimple—such a sad, salty word—she's ageless. I bet she's shopping for refugee families or abused women; people in need.

The nun doesn't dip through the sneaky short-cuts, not like Matty does when he comes with me. *Straight to the end, so they can't sucker you into buying more crap you don't need,* he says. But how do you know if you need it or not if you don't even lay eyes on it? For example, the picture frame shelf? If we had one of those, our wedding portrait wouldn't have crashed off the wall. Maybe stemmed glassware would make us more refined and floral sheets would encourage something to grow.

The nun stops at a decorator bedroom, sits on the edge of the bed and bounces twice. She lays herself down atop of the covers. The bottoms of her black shoes are worn thin. How tired she must be, taking such careful steps, acceding to God's wants and whims. Serving only Him and not herself.

I know I should hurry, that Matty is waiting, but the beds are so inviting and so soft.

About the Author

Sara Hills' short fiction has featured in *SmokeLong Quarterly, Cheap Pop, X-R-A-Y Literary, Fractured Lit, New Flash Fiction Review,* and others. She's won the National Flash Fiction Day micro competition, the Retreat West quarterly competition, and been commended in the Bath Flash Fiction Award. Her work has been nominated for the Pushcart Prize, Best Microfictions, Best Short Fictions, and Best of the Net; included in the BIFFY50; and twice shortlisted for the Bridport Prize. Originally from the Sonoran Desert in Southern Arizona, Sara lives in Warwickshire, UK with her family and tweets from @sarahillswrites. *The Evolution of Birds* is her first book of collected work.

Acknowledgements

The Evolution of Birds would not have been possible without the encouragement and unwavering support of so many kind people.

Thank you, first of all, to Jude Higgins of Ad Hoc Fiction for believing in me and my weird words, for creating a community where flash fiction can thrive, and for running the Flash Fiction Festival which literally changed my life. Thanks also to John of Ad Hoc Fiction for his book-building mastery and to Kaleia Hills for the gorgeous cover artwork.

Immense gratitude to my family and friends, particularly: Emma Norry, for her friendship, contagious optimism and encouragement, and without whom I wouldn't have started writing and submitting flash fiction in 2019; my first readers and stalwart cheerleaders Susan Connor, Kathleen Keenan, Joy and Cherish Smith; my dear friend and flashy-weirdness guru Amy Barnes; the brilliant Marcy Dilworth for long conversations of the heart and her generous offer to proofread—any remaining mistakes are mine; all my wonderful writing friends in Flash it Better, Flash Corral, Biceps by CK, and the Tuesday Group; Thuy Dinh for the sensitivity reading of "A Prayer to Chim Phượng"; and to the supportive flash community on Twitter —I love you guys!

Unending gratitude to Kathy Fish, Christopher Allen, Jude Higgins, Diane Simmons, and Amy Barnes who've so graciously taken the time to read and provide thoughts on this collection, as well as inspired many of these stories in their fantastic workshops and/or by example of their stunning craft. I am so lucky to know you all.

To my children—Sonora, Kaleia, and Fionniain—the greatest treasures in my life and without whom I would be lost, thank you for showing me what freedom feels like; watching you soar has given me wings.

And to Thomas, for always believing in me and keeping my heart safe, a task for which words of thanks will never be enough.

Previously Published

Grateful thanks to the following anthologies and journals where these works were previously published:

This is How it Starts – *Root, Branch, Tree: 2020 National Flash Fiction Day Anthology*, June 2020

Pill Babies – *Restore to Factory Settings: Bath Flash Fiction Volume Five*, Ad Hoc Fiction, December 2020

A Piteraq is an Avalanche of Wind – *Reflex Fiction*, September 2020

How to Tell a Scary Story – *X-R-A-Y Literary Magazine*, April 2021

Always Down a Dirt Road, I'm Walking – *Bath Flash Fiction Award*, Commended, February 2021

Lions in the Amazon – *SmokeLong Quarterly*, September 2020

Safety in Numbers – *Retreat West*, January 2020

Catch and Release – *Root, Branch, Tree: 2020 National Flash Fiction Day Anthology*, June 2020

Girls of Summer – *Retreat West*, March 2021

From Within the Juniper – *Reflex Fiction*, May 2020

A Baby Born En Caul Can Never Drown – *Janus Literary*, May 2021

Women Get Hungry – *One Eye on the Cows: Bath Flash Fiction Volume Four*, Ad Hoc Fiction, December 2019

Ewe – *Cease, Cows*, May 2021

Osmosis – *Reckon Review*, April 2021

Public Transportation – *NFFD FlashFlood*, June 2020

Each Breath a Chain – *Janus Literary*, February 2021

When the Girl on Seventh Avenue Offers You a Mango – *Retreat West*, Monthly Micro Competition Shortlist, July 2020

Knock Loudly and Wait – *Retreat West*, Monthly Micro Competition Shortlist, May 2020

Home Improvement – *Reflex Fiction*, July 2019

Some Things Never Change – *Paragraph Planet*, February 2021

On Ten Bay Beach – *National Flash Fiction Day New Zealand (Micro Madness)*, June 2020

Here is the Church – *NFFD FlashFlood*, June 2019

The Hill We Die On – *Janus Literary*, February 2021

When Neil Armstrong Walks on the Moon – *National Flash Fiction Day*, March 2020 and *Root, Branch, Tree: 2020 National Flash Fiction Day Anthology*, June 2020

Havasu Falls – *National Flash Fiction Day*, April 2019; *And We Pass Through: 2019 National Flash Fiction Day Anthology*, June 2019

Lunar Landing – *New Flash Fiction Review*, April 2021

Waxing After Waning – *One Eye on the Cows: Bath Flash Fiction Volume Four*, Ad Hoc Fiction, December 2019

On the Night of Miracles – *Retreat West*, Monthly Micro Competition Shortlist, June 2020

Holy Jesus, There's a Nun in IKEA – *CHEAP POP*, September 2020